Th Wondaglop Plot

Harriet Castor

Illustrated by Terry Mckenna

Hodder
Children's
Books

a division of Hodder Headline plc

To J.B.
Harriet Castor

Text copyright © Harriet Castor 1995
Illustrations copyright © Terry McKenna 1995

First published in Great Britain in 1995
by Hodder Children's Books

A Catalogue record for this book is available from the British Library

ISBN 0 340 63442 1

Printed and bound in Great Britain by
Cox & Wyman Ltd, Reading, Berks.

Hodder Children's Books
A Division of Hodder Headline PLC
338 Euston Road
London NW1 3BH

CHAPTER ONE

What is the connection
between Joe Burger
(trainee supersleuth)

a pot of face cream

and a tiny island in the
middle of the Specific
Ocean?

You don't know?
Nor did Joe Burger.
But he was about to
find out.

Because on that island, miles from anywhere, a scientist called Professor Floral Powderpuff had just made a discovery.

She had found that if you took the sticky stuff that came out of one sort of tree, and mixed it with the oozy stuff that came out of another sort of tree, then added some of the sludgy stuff from around a nearby pond . . .

you got the most amazing face cream.

More than amazing - it was the most exciting, fantastic, incredible face cream that there had ever been.

Because when you put it on, anyone who looked at you saw, not you, but their own vision of the best, cleverest, loveliest person in the world. And so, of course, everyone thought you were their hero.

Professor Powderpuff made lots of this special mixture, put it in pots, and called it Wondaglop.

Then she put adverts for Wondaglop in lots of newspapers around the world.

And as the orders came flooding in to the tiny island in the middle of the Specific Ocean . . .

. . . the crates of Wondaglop went flooding out.

But then one Tuesday, Professsor Powderpuff discovered that while there was plenty of sticky stuff left in the sticky trees, and plenty of oozy stuff left in the oozy trees, there was hardly any sludgy stuff left around the pond. She tried just putting the sticky stuff and the oozy stuff together, but it was no good. So that is how there came to be an advert in the *Netherbottom Ridge Bugle* newspaper for the last ever crate of Wondaglop.

And after he'd seen the advert, and decided that Wondaglop was just what he needed, that is how the last ever crate came to be delivered, one Saturday morning, to the house of Bad-Breath Bernie.

CHAPTER TWO

That same morning, somewhere else
in Netherbottom Ridge, Joe Burger
was still in bed, having the sort of
dream that only great supersleuths
can have. He had just cracked the
most cunning code ever invented, and
saved the world . . .

. . . when his mother decided to try
out her new megaphone.

Joe woke up. He made a face under the duvet. Life in the Burger household hadn't been quite the same recently. The thing was, there was about to be an election for a new town mayor, and Joe's mother had decided to stand.

She'd seen the advert in the paper, and had decided that it was the *perfect* job for her.

ELECTIONS FOR MAYOR

YOU COULD BE A CANDIDATE!

WINNER GETS ~
☆   BIG HOUSE
    LONG SHINY CAR
LOTS OF PARTY INVITATIONS
    ☆   ☆   ☆

(MUST ALSO BE PREPARED
TO PLANT TREES, UNVEIL
PLAQUES AND LAUNCH BOATS.)

The present mayor, Mr Cribbins, was retiring. He was 92 and had been re-elected for the past 47 years on the trot.

Now he was fed up with parties, thought the car was a silly shape, and rather fancied a medium sized bungalow.

Joe's mother was taking her campaign seriously. The latest thing was her new megaphone, which she put on top of the car. It made it a bit embarrassing when you were trying to learn your spellings on the way to school.

The election was getting Joe down. But even worse, it was keeping him from his supersleuthing. He hadn't solved a case in months. Not even a tiny one.

Because as soon as he got home from school every day, he and Dog, his sleuthing assistant, were kept busy licking envelopes, and delivering leaflets and putting up posters until bedtime.

Sometimes they got so tired that they found themselves delivering posters, licking leaflets and putting up envelopes.

It was getting beyond a joke.

CHAPTER THREE

Joe's mother was doing rather well, and it looked as if she might win the election. This was probably because the only other two candidates were hopeless.

One of them was Colin Smallbody, the greengrocer, who was campaigning with the slogan *"Cabbages are people too"*. As this plainly wasn't true, Colin wasn't getting much support.

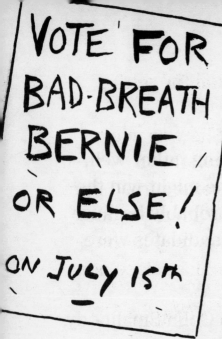

VOTE FOR BAD-BREATH BERNIE / OR ELSE!

ON JULY 15ᵗʰ

The other candidate was Bad-Breath Bernie.

Bad-Breath Bernie used to be a crook. He had once robbed the Netherbottom Ridge Bank. He hadn't used a gun - he had overpowered the cashier just by breathing on her. But then he'd been arrested on the bus on the way home by an off-duty policeman with no sense of smell.

When he got out of prison, he saw the advert for a new mayor. This set him thinking, and soon he had a new plan for getting rich.

He decided that if he was mayor he would sell off the whole of Netherbottom Ridge to be turned into a great big car park. With the money, he'd buy lots of cars to keep in the car park, and he'd build a palace next door to live in.

At first he thought it would be easy to win the election. But, even with a clean vest and a multipack of breath freshener, people didn't seem too keen on him.

So when he saw the advert in the Netherbottom Ridge Bugle for the last ever crate of Wondaglop, the face cream that makes you a hero, he knew it was just what he needed.

18

CHAPTER FOUR

A few days later, Mr Burger was surprised to see in the paper that Bad-Breath Bernie had pulled out of the election campaign, and that a new candidate had taken his place.

Anthony Etherbridge-Plonk! Who on earth is that?

What's more, when Joe and Dog went delivering leaflets, all everyone could talk about was this mysterious Mr Plonk.

After a few days, the whole Burger family had had quite enough of listening to people going on and on about Mr Plonk.

"I want to see him for myself," said Mrs Burger. "I'm not going to be pipped to the post by some upstart puppy pipsqueak!"

So when the Netherbottom Ridge Bugle announced that Mr Plonk was going to open the new fishfinger counter at the local supermarket, the Burgers decided to go along.

When they got to the Stockitall Store, they found that the rest of Netherbottom Ridge had turned out too. Soon, in a blaze of flash-bulbs, Mr Plonk arrived.

Everyone stared.

"He's so dashing . . . and
glamorous . . . just like a
film star," said
Mrs Burger.

"Glamorous?" said Mr Burger.
"What are you talking about?"

"He looks like a good, solid golfing sort of chap to me, with a definite interest in bird watching."

"They're *both* talking rubbish!" thought Joe. "That man's a great detective, it's obvious."

Dog was just wondering why he'd never seen a giant bone wearing an overcoat before.

Anthony Etherbridge-Plonk kissed some babies, shook hands with some grannies, and signed lots of autographs.

By the time he had left, everyone was hopelessly in love, and swearing that they would vote for him in the elections. Even Mrs Burger.

"But you're standing against him, my dear!" said Mr Burger.

She *didn't* care!

CHAPTER FIVE

An hour later, back at his house, Bad-Breath Bernie was washing his face and chuckling to himself.

Back at the Burgers', Joe was very excited. He couldn't stop thinking about Mr Plonk. At last he'd found the supersleuthing hero who would teach him everything he needed to know. He could picture it now: every evening after school, he would sit at Mr Plonk's feet, hearing tales of past cases solved, and helping him sift through the clues for his latest mystery.

Standing in the mayor's elections was clearly just a cover for Mr Plonk's real work in Netherbottom. What could it be? Perhaps there was some big case going on!

Joe had to find out. There was no time to waste. He grabbed his autograph book, and set off. When he got to the street where Mr Plonk lived, he saw a crowd outside his house. There was even a TV crew.

Two men were standing by the front door.

Joe thought they didn't look terribly friendly, so he decided to nip round the back instead.

The alley along the side of the house was muddy and full of litter, and just as Joe rounded the corner he slipped on a crisp packet, slithered on something slimy, and ended up head down in Mr Plonk's dustbin.

CHAPTER SIX

It was dark inside the dustbin, and rather smelly. But Joe thought he'd stay there for a minute or two. Even his hero's rubbish was important. It might teach him what *he* should be throwing away too.

There were scrunched up wrappers and cartons and bits of string. There were apple cores and banana skins and nasty looking pieces of rind.

There was a pair of old slippers that were particularly smelly. And there was lots of crumpled paper. One bit of paper in particular caught Joe's eye. He could only see a few squiggles on it, but those squiggles were familiar. They were his father's writing.

Joe wriggled out of the dustbin, and grabbed the letter. It was an invitation to Mr Plonk to join the Netherbottom Ridge Golf Club!

"Blimey, Dad must like him," said Joe.

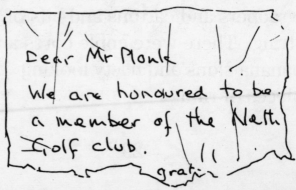

Dear Mr Plonk
We are honoured to be
a member of the Neth
Golf club.
                    grati

The dustbin seemed to be full of lots of other letters, too. Joe looked at them. They were fan letters from all sorts of people.

The strange thing was that everyone seemed to have a very different idea of what Mr Plonk was like.

Then Joe spotted something else, underneath the letters. It was a small shiny pot.

He picked it up and read the label.

wondaglop

THE FACE CREAM

THAT MAKES YOU A HERO

There was some small print on the back. Joe studied it for a moment. Then he stuffed all the letters and the pot into his coat and ran home.

Somehow, his mother guessed that he'd spent part of the afternoon upside down with his head in a dustbin, so she put him straight in the bath.

Later, back in his supersleuth's
HQ, Joe got out the letters and spread
them on the floor. Then he read the
Wondaglop label again. He looked in
the pot. There was a last blob in the
bottom corner. He rubbed it on his
face.

Suddenly, Dog jumped on him in a
frenzy of licking.

Two seconds later, Joe's face was Wondaglop free, and Dog had a very funny taste on his tongue.

Don't know what came over me!

Joe wiped the dog-lick off his face, and the terrible truth began to dawn on him.

Mr Plonk wasn't a great supersleuth at all, any more than he was a master hairdresser or a champion golfer. But who was he? Joe checked the calendar. The election was tomorrow! He was going to have to find out - fast.

CHAPTER SEVEN

The next morning, Joe had to do some last minute emergency leafletting for his mother.

So it was the afternoon before he could get back to Mr Plonk's house. He went straight down the alley, avoiding the crisp packets and the slimy stuff. Then he crept his way up the garden. The back door was locked, but there was a window open, and Joe climbed in.

By the awful sounds coming from the bathroom, it sounded like Mr Plonk - whoever he was - was in the bath.

"Now's my chance," thought Joe, quickly.

Joe crept up the stairs, and found Mr Plonk's bedroom. There, on the dressing table, was a full pot of Wondaglop.

Joe picked it up.

Just then the bathroom door opened.

Quickly stuffing the Wondaglop into his pocket, Joe leapt into the wardrobe.

Peering out through the slits in the door, he saw a pair of hairy feet, with nasty yellow toenails . . .

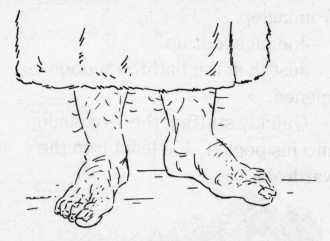

. . . attached to a pair of very hairy legs . . . attached to a large towel . . . attached to . . . Bad-Breath Bernie!

Surely *he* couldn't be Mr Plonk? Bad-Breath Bernie was searching the dressing-table.

"Stew my socks!" he was saying, "I could have sworn . . . Oh well, plenty more where that came from."

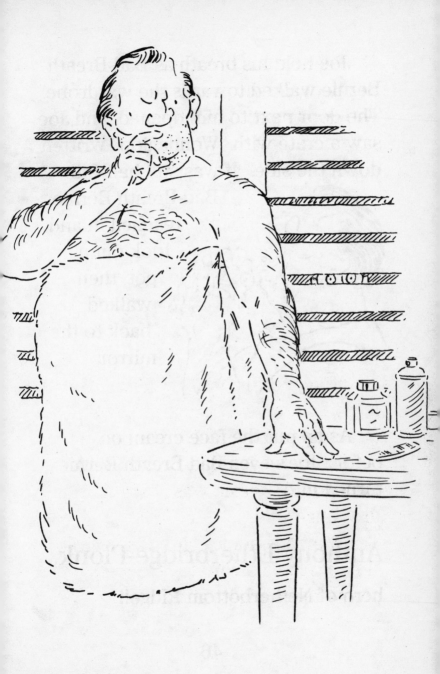

Joe held his breath as Bad-Breath Bernie walked towards the wardrobe. The door next to him opened, and Joe saw a crate with "Wondaglop" written down the side. It was still half-full.

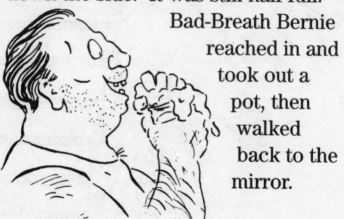 Bad-Breath Bernie reached in and took out a pot, then walked back to the mirror.

As he put the face cream on, before Joe's eyes Bad-Breath Bernie turned into

Anthony Etherbridge-Plonk,

hero of Netherbottom Ridge!!

"Well matey," Plonk said to himself, still in Bad-Breath Bernie's voice, "tonight you'll be mayor. Then you can start on your plan. Soon Netherbottom will be one big car park and you'll be rich, rich, rich!"

And with that, he left the room.

CHAPTER EIGHT

Joe heard Bad-Breath Bernie shut the front door behind him. An "Ooh!" and an "Aah!" went up from the crowd outside.

Joe's head was in a spin so he stayed in the wardrobe for a while to calm down. When he eventually got out, he came downstairs, climbed out of the window, and sat on the back doorstep to think.

Netherbottom Ridge a car park - what on earth did he mean?

Whatever Bad-Breath Bernie's plan was, it sounded nasty. Joe had to stop him. But how?

He couldn't stop the election - the voting was almost finished already. Soon everyone would gather in the town hall, the election results would be read out, and Bad-Breath Bernie - safely disguised in Wondaglop - would be the new mayor!

Joe shuddered at the thought. He couldn't just *tell* people what he knew - who would believe him? He must have proof.

He looked at his watch - and jumped. It was six o'clock. The town hall meeting was in just half an hour.

Joe paced up and down. He needed an idea - and quickly.

Then he spotted something in the flowerbeds. All at once his eyes lit up.

It was a garden hose. He rolled it up as fast as he could, and staggered off down the road.

As Joe neared the town hall, people were already arriving for the meeting. Swerving into Mrs Petunia's garden next door, he fixed the end of the hose to her garden tap. Then he stuck Dog's collar to it. It was a special collar with a magnet for working the dog-flap on the front door.

Joe told Dog his clever plan.

"When I wiggle the hose like this you turn it on. OK?"

Then Joe jogged backwards across the grass, unwinding the hose.

He unwound it out through the gate, onto the pavement, round the corner, and up the Town Hall steps.

Tearing through the entrance hall, he crept in between the thick forest of legs in the meeting room.

As Joe squeezed and shoved, Mr Sprog was solemnly reading out the voting results.

Meanwhile, back in Mrs Petunia's garden, Dog - who was settling down to sleep - had been spotted by Boris, Mrs Petunia's cat. Boris didn't like dogs.

Joe tunnelled his way to the front of the crowd. He edged over to where Mr Plonk was standing, then he wiggled the hose . . . which was the signal for Dog to turn the tap on.

And just at that moment, Boris spat . . . crouched . . . and leapt at Dog. Dog leapt the other way, and yanked so hard that, quite by chance, he pulled the tap full on.

Dog raced off with Boris in hot
pursuit, and the water gushed along
the hose on the lawn,

to the hose on the pavement,

up the steps,

through the entrance hall
and in between the legs of the people
all crowding forward to hear what Mr
Sprog was saying.

"Anthony Etherbridge-Plonk
(Anthony Etherbridge-Plonk Party),
7992 votes . . ."

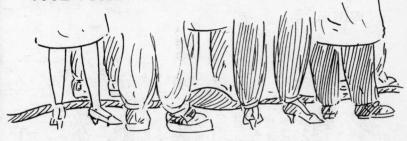

Joe pointed the nozzle straight up,
and . . .

nothing happened.

Joe desperately wiggled the hose
again. Nothing. He peered along the
floor, in amongst all the feet, and saw
what the trouble was. The butcher,
Mr Cleaver, was standing on the hose.
Behind him, the water was building
up so much that the hose was
blowing up like a balloon.

Joe just had time to shout:

"Mr Cleaver! Look ou–"
when . . .

The hose burst, blasting Mr Cleaver high into the air on a great gush of water.

Mr Sprog was still talking, ". . . I hereby declare the new mayor— oh no ! ! !"

Down came the water, and down came Mr Cleaver, landing on top of his wife, who was holding little George. The baby shot out of her hands and flew in a perfect curve up towards the ceiling.

The crowd gasped, and then everything went deadly quiet.

But Fred Mudthump, captain of the Netherbottom Amateur Rugby Club (who could have turned professional if it hadn't been for his flat feet) was already running backwards, arms outstretched.

Making a perfect curve down again, the baby plopped safely into his hands. Resisting the urge to drop-kick him over the chandelier, Fred stumbled backwards into the wall, straight onto a little box marked

SPRINKLER SYSTEM
- IN CASE OF FIRE
- FOR EMERGENCY
  USE ONLY

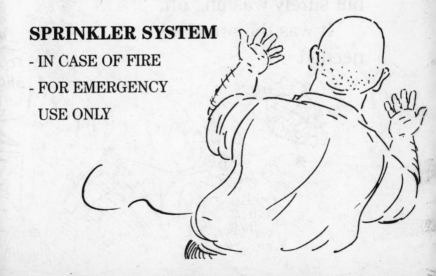

All at once there was the most incredible indoor downpour. People reached for their brollies - and found that they hadn't brought them. Joe - who'd been so worried about Baby Cleaver that he'd forgotten all about his master plan - looked up, and laughed.

For there, in front of the whole of Netherbottom Ridge, Anthony Etherbridge-Plonk's Wondaglop cream was slowly but surely washing off.

It was the proof he needed.

"It's Bad-Breath Bernie!" someone shouted, and everyone turned and stared.

CHAPTER NINE

Now they knew Mr Plonk was actually Bad-Breath Bernie, everyone said there'd been something fishy about him all along.

Mr Sprog announced that the election would be held again the next day, and the whole town was greatly relieved, except for Mrs Blight, who was going to have to count the votes all over again.

When the new results were announced, Joe's mother had won by a mile, and a week later the Burger family packed all their things into boxes and moved into a very big house.

Joe liked the house. It had an extra-big room for his supersleuth's HQ.

He liked the long shiny car too.
Except that his mother insisted on
keeping the megaphone on the roof

as a memento, so everyone still knew
how bad Joe was at spelling!

As for the Wondaglop, the police took away all the pots in Bad-Breath Bernie's house.

And since his had been the last ever crate of it in the world, that was the end of the matter.

Except that a few days later, Dog was on his way home past the police station when he had an accident with the dustbin.

And no matter how many baths he had, he was never quite the same again.

h HODDER Another Read Alone from
Hodder Children's Books

JAM SPONGE AND SNEAKERS
A Joe Burger Mystery

Harriet Castor

Joe Burger's father wants him to be a
tightrope walker. His mum wants him
to be an astronaut. But Joe's going to
be a supersleuth.
The greatest detective ever!

Jam sponge pudding – YUK!
Nobody minds when it goes missing
from school. But to Joe Burger it
means only one thing – the dreaded
Cake Shop Gang are in town! Is Joe
Burger sneaky enough to stop their
sticky plans, or will he get stuck in
the pudding?

**Another Read Alone from
Hodder Children's Books**

MOTORWAY MADNESS

Kathy Henderson

Where would you go on *your* dream
holiday? Disneyland or darkest
Africa?

Amil doesn't even *want* a holiday, but
nobody's giving him the choice.

It's not until motorway madness takes
over that the real fun can begin ...

0 340 63441 3	JAM SPONGE AND SNEAKERS *Harriet Castor*	£2.99 ☐
0 340 63446 4	MOTORWAY MADNESS *Kathy Henderson*	£2.99 ☐
0 340 62675 5	THE BOFFIN *Lisa Taylor and Tony Blundell*	£2.99 ☐

All these books are available at your local bookshop or newsagent, or can be ordered direct from the publisher. Just tick the titles you want and fill in the form below.

Prices and availability subject to change without notice.

Hodder Children's Books,
Cash Sales Department,
Bookpoint, 39 Milton Park,
Abingdon, Oxon OX14 4TD, UK.

If you have a credit card you may order by telephone. Our direct line is 01235 400414 (lines open 9.00 am – 6.00 pm Monday to Saturday, 24 hour message answering service). Alternatively you can send a fax on 01235 400454.

Or please send cheque or postal order for the value of the book, and add the following for postage and packing:

U.K. INCLUDING B.F.P.O. – £1.00 for one book, plus 50p for the second book, and 30p for each additional book ordered up to a £3.00 maximum.

OVERSEAS INCLUDING EIRE – £2.00 for the first book, plus £1.00 for the second book, and 50p for each additional book ordered.

OR Please debit this amount from my Access/Visa Card (delete as appropriate).

Card Number ☐☐☐☐☐☐☐☐☐☐☐☐☐☐☐☐

Amount £ ....

Expiry Date ....

Signed ....

Name ....

Address ....